BRAVE DAVE

For Coco, with love —G.A.
To Arthur —G.P-R.

Text copyright © 2022 by Giles Andreae
Illustrations copyright © 2022 by Guy Parker-Rees

Brave Dave was first published in the United Kingdom in 2022 by The Watts Publishing Group.

ISBN 978-1-338-86133-4

10 9 8 7 6 5 4 3 2 1   22 23 24 25 26

Printed in the U.S.A.   76
This edition first printing, September 2022

BRAVE DAVE

GILES ANDREAE

GUY PARKER-REES

SCHOLASTIC INC.

Clarence was **MIGHTY** and Clarence was **STRONG**.

He was handsome and tall; he was **BRAVE**.

He was everything grizzly bears ought to be,

And then there was . . .

Then there was **DAVE**.

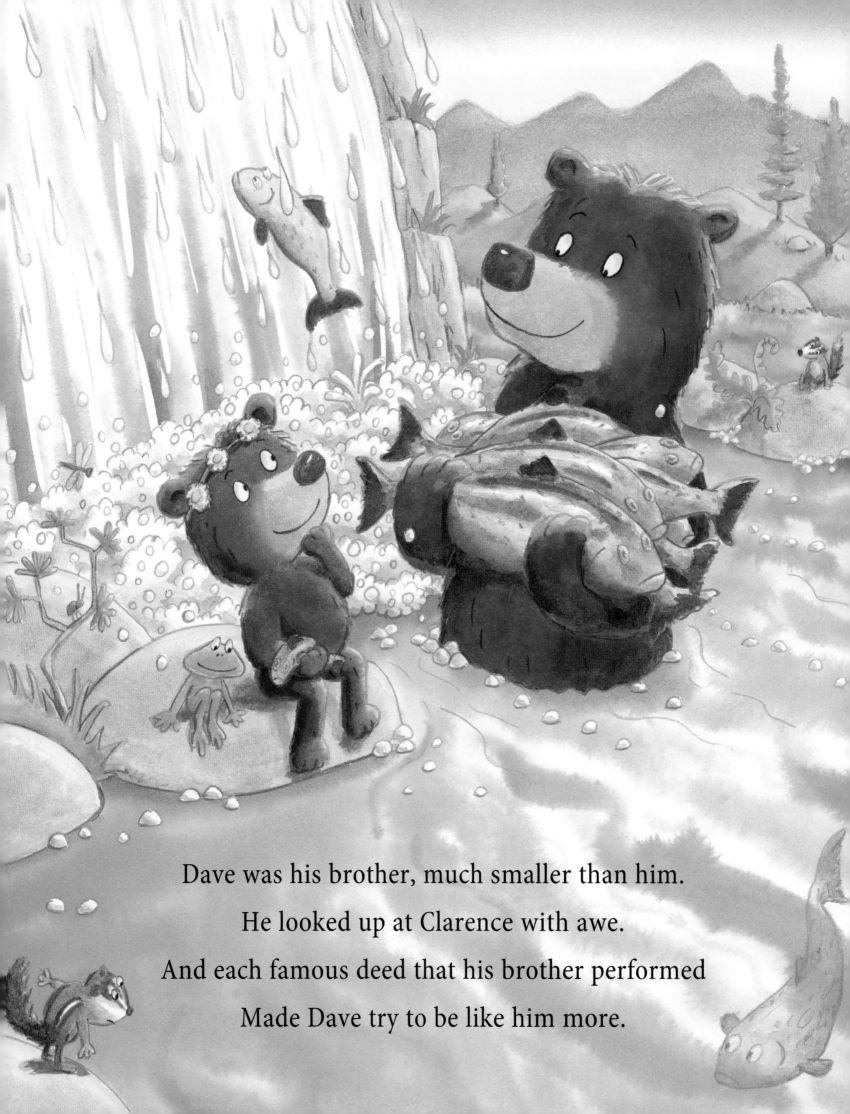

Dave was his brother, much smaller than him.

He looked up at Clarence with awe.

And each famous deed that his brother performed

Made Dave try to be like him more.

"Like **THIS**, Dave!
Like **THAT**, Dave!"
said Clarence.
"Come on!

Keep going and
someday you'll see . . .

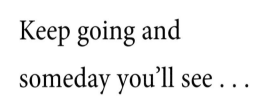

That if you do
everything just how I say
You'll end up as brave
as, well . . . **ME!**"

Dave tried his best to do everything right,
But one day, he started to cry.

"I'll never be Clarence, not **EVER!**" he sniffed,
As he gazed at the darkening sky.

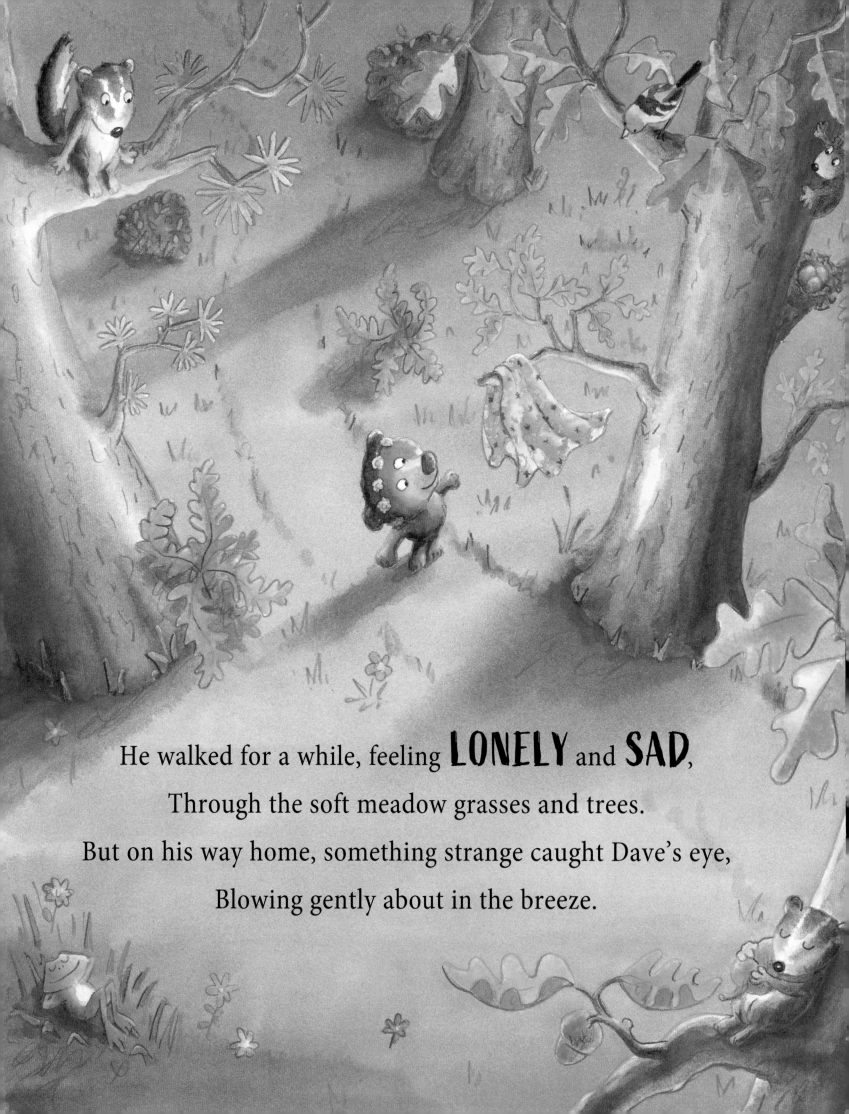

He walked for a while, feeling **LONELY** and **SAD**,

Through the soft meadow grasses and trees.

But on his way home, something strange caught Dave's eye,

Blowing gently about in the breeze.

As soon as he held it, Dave felt his **HEART SOAR;**
The patterns, the colors so bright.
It lifted his soul like the far-distant stars
That he loved to watch twinkle at night.

The very next day, Dave began picking flowers
Of all sorts of colors and hues;
Bright sunny yellows and deep berry reds,
Pinks, purples, and luminous blues.

He didn't see Clarence, his brother, at all.

He kept out of everyone's way,

Retreating most nights to the depths of his cave,

Afraid of the things they might say.

"I reckon he's keeping a secret in there,"
Said a chipmunk, "but what can it be?"

"It sounds like he's busy with something, for sure.

Keep still and perhaps we might see!"

Then one day, Dave felt like his heart might **EXPLODE**,
And he knew he was left with no choice.

So he called all the animals
there to his den,

And he spoke in a
trembling voice.

"I'm just not the same as the others," he said
As he stood at the mouth of the cave.
"I'm **NOT** very strong and I'm **NOT** very tough,
And I'm certainly **NOT** very brave.

But there's something that makes me feel happy at last;
That finally makes me feel . . . **TRUE**."

And he held out a gift for his brother to take.
"I made it," Dave said. "It's for **YOU**."

The cloak was the color of wild mountain skies,

Of the valleys, the rivers . . . the birds.

And all the animals stood there amazed,

As they waited for Clarence's words.

"You **MADE** it . . . ?" said Clarence.

"You made it for **ME?**"

"I did," Dave replied, "look, with these."

And he showed him the colors

He'd mixed from the flowers

And the threads from the grasses and trees.

"I've never seen anything like it," said Clarence.
"It's just . . . it's so **BEAUTIFUL**, Dave!
And to speak with such honesty, straight from your heart,
Well that, let me tell you . . . **THAT'S BRAVE**.

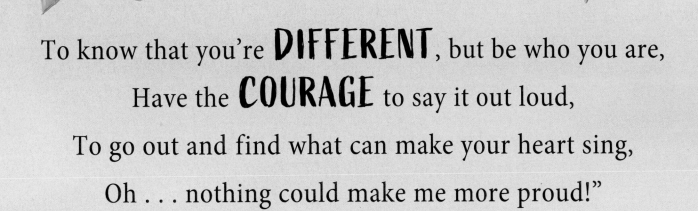

To know that you're **DIFFERENT**, but be who you are,
Have the **COURAGE** to say it out loud,
To go out and find what can make your heart sing,
Oh . . . nothing could make me more proud!"

Dave felt his body collapse with relief,
And the animals started to cheer.

"Then come with me, everyone, quickly!" said Dave.

"I think you might like it in here!"

The animals followed Dave into his den,
And couldn't believe what they saw.
It was filled with the patterns and colors and shades
Of the **MAGICAL LAND** they adored;

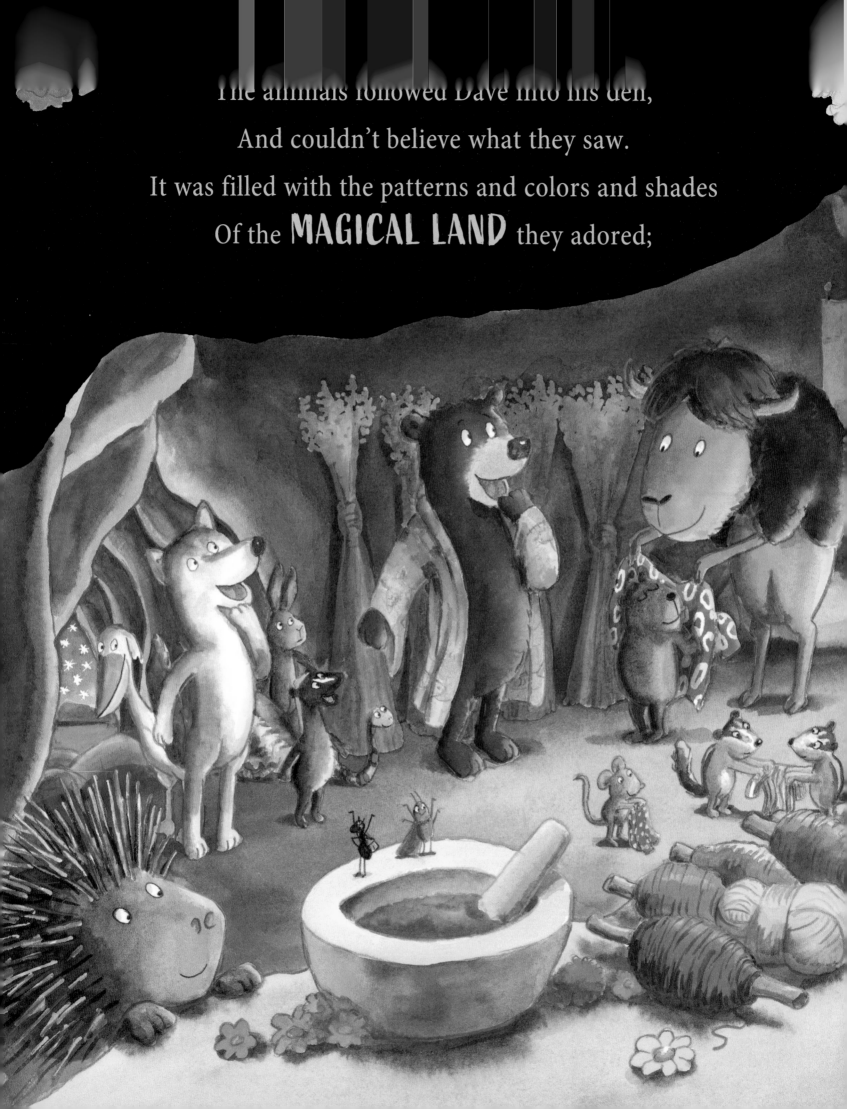

Turquoises, oranges, crimsons, and greens;

Stripes, circles, and stars shining bright.

The animals each chose a robe for themselves . . .

And paraded **LONG** into the night.

And now, if you go to the forest yourself,

Please don't be surprised if you see

A grizzly or two dressed in

DAZZLING CLOTHES...

Looking happy as

HAPPY CAN BE!